86145

MINERVA LOUISE

at School

Janet Morgan Stoeke

Dutton Children's Books
NEW YORK

For my mom and dad with love

Copyright © 1996 by Janet Morgan Stoeke

Library of Congress Cataloging-in-Publication Data

Stoeke, Janet Morgan.
Minerva Louise at school/Janet Morgan Stoeke
[author and illustrator].—1st ed.
p. cm.
Summary: Out for an early morning walk, a chicken
wanders into a school that she mistakes for a fancy barn.
ISBN 0-525-45494-2
[1. Schools—Fiction.   2. Chickens—Fiction.]   I. Title.
PZ7.S869Mk   1996
[E]—dc20   95-52173   CIP   AC

Published in the United States 1996 by Dutton Children's Books,
a division of Penguin Books USA Inc.
375 Hudson Street, New York, New York 10014
Printed in Hong Kong   First Edition
10 9 8 7 6 5 4 3 2 1

One morning, Minerva Louise woke up
before everyone else.

It was a beautiful morning, so she decided
to go for a walk through the tall grass.

She walked on and on.

Oh, look! A big, fancy barn,
thought Minerva Louise.

She watched the farmer hang
his laundry out to dry . . .

. . . and she noticed that he had left the door open.

So many stalls! There must be
all kinds of animals here.

Here are milking stools for the cows

and a pen for the pigs.

Oh, a bucket, too. It must be
for feeding the chickens.

Nesting boxes! How wonderful!

Look at them all. And each one
is decorated differently.

This one is all done up with ribbons.

And this one is lined with fur.

Oh my goodness, there's an EGG in this one!

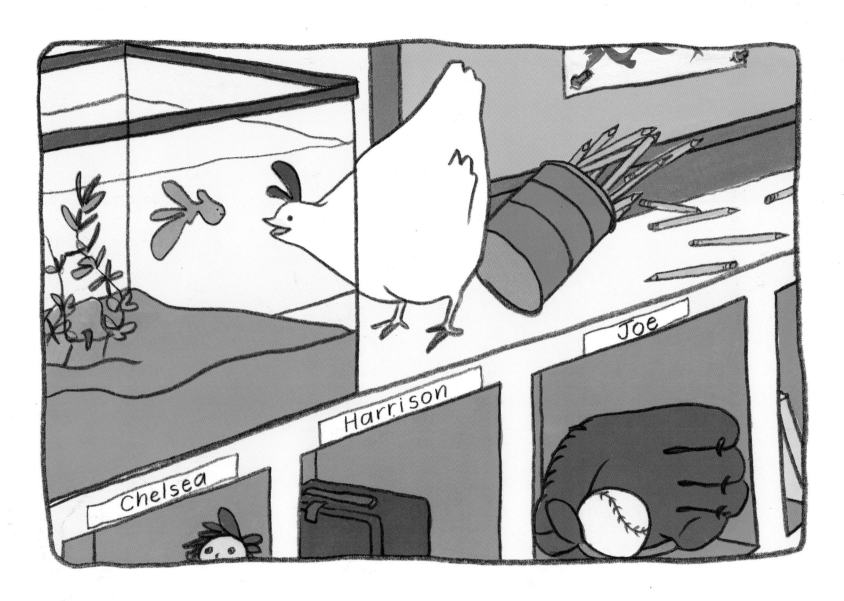

But where is his mother? He'll get cold.

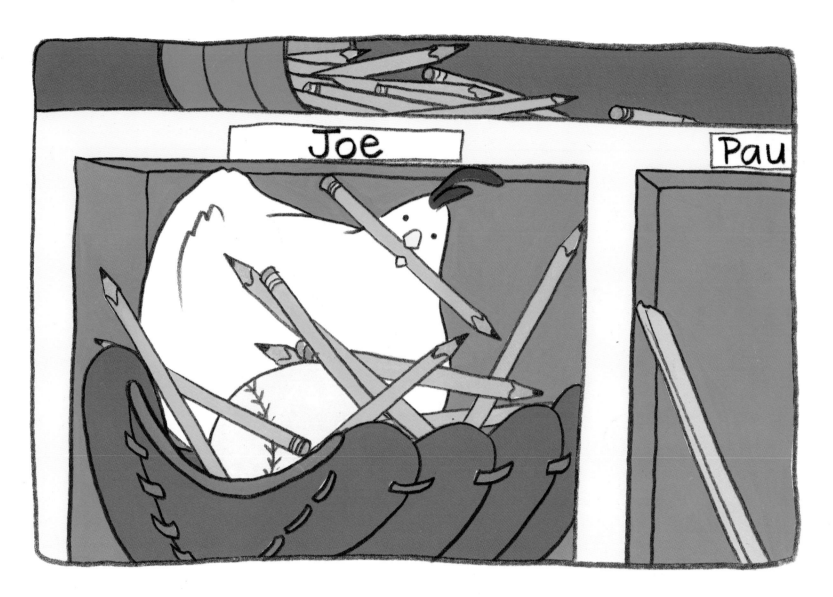

Well, this hay will keep you warm.

I'm sure the animals are around here somewhere. But I have to go home now.

Minerva Louise hurried home
through the tall grass.

She had some work to do.

But she knew she'd go back to the
fancy barn some day . . .

because it was such a wonderful
place to get new ideas.